LITTLE RED RIDING HOOD

Retold by Heather Amery

Illustrated by Stephen Cartwright

Language consultant: Betty Root

Series editor: Jenny Tyler

There's a little yellow duck to find on every page.

This is Little Red Riding Hood and her mother.

They live near a big, dark forest. Her name comes from
a bright red cloak with a hood that her Granny made her.

"Please take this food to your Granny."

"She's poorly in bed," says her mother. "Go through the forest but don't talk to any strangers you meet on the way."

Little Red Riding Hood waves goodbye.

She walks into the forest with her basket. She doesn't see the Big Black Wolf watching her from behind a tree.

Suddenly the Wolf is on the path.

"Where are you going?" he asks. "I'm taking this food to my Granny," says Red Riding Hood, feeling very scared.

The Wolf smiles a horrible smile.

"Take your Granny some flowers," he says. Red Riding Hood is even more scared. "Yes, Mr. Wolf," she says.

Red Riding Hood stops to pick some flowers.

The Wolf smiles again showing his sharp teeth. Then he runs away through the forest. He is very, very hungry.

The Wolf reaches Granny's cottage.

Granny is sitting up in bed. The Wolf pushes open the door and runs in. He gobbles up Granny in one gulp.

He climbs into Granny's bed.

He puts on her night cap and glasses. He pulls up the quilt
and waits for Red Riding Hood to come.

Red Riding Hood knocks on Granny's door.

"It's me, Granny," she says. "Come in, my dear," calls the
Wolf in a squeaky voice. "I'm in my bedroom."

"Hello, Granny," says Red Riding Hood.

Then she stares. "What big eyes you've got," she says.

"All the better to see you with," squeaks the Wolf.

"What big ears you've got," says Red Riding Hood.

"All the better to hear you with," squeaks the Wolf.

Red Riding Hood drops her flowers. She is very scared indeed.

"What big teeth you've got," she says.

"All the better to eat you with." Red Riding Hood screams but the Wolf gobbles her up. Then he gets back into bed.

A woodsman hears the scream.

He runs as fast as he can to the cottage. He goes in the door and straight into Granny's bedroom.

He sees the Wolf and kills it.

Inside the Wolf are Red Riding Hood and her Granny.

They are alive and very happy to be rescued.

"Thank you for saving us," says Granny.

"The Wolf can never scare anyone again." And they all
sit down at the table to have cake and coffee.

This edition first published in 2003 by Usborne Publishing Ltd, 83-85 Saffron Hill, London EC1N 8RT, England. www.usborne.com
Copyright © 2003, 1996 Usborne Publishing Ltd.
The name Usborne and the devices ♀ 🌐 are Trade Marks of Usborne Publishing Ltd. All rights reserved. No part of this publication may be reproduced,
stored in a retrieval system, or transmitted in any form or by any means, electronic, mechanical, photocopying, recording
or otherwise, without prior permission of the publisher. UE. This edition first published in America in 2004. Printed in Belgium.